STINKERBELL

AND THE FRIDGE FAIRIES

J.J. MURHALL

Illustrated by Tony Blundell

BLOOMSBURY

This book is dedicated to
Michael, Saoirse Ruby and Alfie
with *loads* of love.
And to all the 'Little Stinkers' everywhere
who are 'still dreaming'.

(A *very* special thank you also to
Helen Cross and Eric Dupin.)

First published in Great Britain in 1997
Bloomsbury Publishing Plc, 38 Soho Square, London W1V 5DF

ISBN 0 7475 3288 5 (paperback)
ISBN 0 7475 3287 7 (hardback)

Printed and bound in Great Britain by Clays Ltd, St Ives Plc

10 9 8 7 6 5 4 3 2 1

The Gobs
Come Calling

STINKERBELL STOOD in the middle of the school playground and stamped her foot.

'DOUGLAS!' she roared at the top of her tiny voice, 'if you don't stop following me around, I shall not, I repeat *not* be responsible for my actions.'

The little pixie eyed Stinkerbell and her TV aerial wand suspiciously and scribbled something down in a notebook.

Stinkerbell snatched it out of his hand. 'What's this?' she asked, waving it under his nose. 'Taking down notes about me now? Honestly, Douglas, I thought you wanted to be in charge of the compost heap, not a private detective.'

Douglas looked at her indignantly. 'You know the King told me to keep an eye on you, Stinkerbell. If you want to stay down at the bottom of the garden for good this time, you're just going to have to put up with it. Now. What's it to be? Do you want to go back in the dustbin, Stinkerbell? Because it can be arranged.' Douglas peered seriously at her over the top of his round spectacles.

Stinkerbell pulled a face at him and took another peek at the notebook. She'd lost count of the number of times the King had uttered the words: 'GET BACK IN THAT BIN!' but this time she'd actually managed two whole weeks without being banished.

She stamped her foot. 'I can't believe what you've written about me,' she said sulkily. '9.05 am. Stinkerbell late for class. Made up excuse about alarm clock not going off. But everyone knows she can't even tell the time.'

Stinkerbell glared at Douglas and then continued: '10.00am: spells and spelling lesson. Stinkerbell not paying attention. Staring out of the window with dreamy look on *her face. 10.30: playtime. Saw Stinkerbell steal sandwich from Ursula's lunchbox.'*

Stinkerbell was furious. 'Huh! I did *not* steal that sandwich, I *borrowed* it. Ursula is a kind and generous pixie and she said that because I don't have a mum or dad to make me a packed lunch, I could borrow one of hers any time I was feeling a bit peckish.'

Douglas didn't look convinced. He was used to Stinkerbell and her tall tales. 'How can you *borrow* a sandwich?' he asked, frowning at her. 'When you borrow something you know that you must always give it back. Unless you're Dwayne and Elvis Gob, of course,' he added with a shudder, remembering the time he was kidnapped by the dreadful Gob family, the meanest and nastiest of all the goblins in the neighbourhood.

'Do you remember when they stole my hankie and never gave it back, Stinkerbell?' said Douglas, who was a sensitive soul, as all pixies tend to be. He sniffed, and looked at Stinkerbell tear-fully. 'I really miss blowing my nose on that handker-chief.'

Stinkerbell stared at him haughtily, and handed him back his notebook. Then she stomped off in her hefty boots towards the climbing frame. She was beginning to think that life in the dustbin was better than having Douglas sticking to her like superglue. At least she'd get some privacy.

She leant against the bars and pulled Ursula's sandwich from her jacket pocket. It was very grubby and covered in bits of old fluff and gritty fairy dust, but Stinkerbell didn't mind. She was used to all things filthy, being the dirtiest, scruffiest fairy around, and besides, it was her favourite – banana and sugar. All fairies have a sweet tooth, but Stinkerbell had the sweetest teeth of all.

She had just stuffed it into her mouth when she saw

the two unmistakable figures of Dwayne and Elvis Gob striding towards her across the playground. They looked as horrible as ever, dressed all in black, with their enormous quiffs, long pointy shoes and rotten old teeth.

''ere, Stinkerbell. You still smell of bananas, then,' declared Elvis Gob, sniffing the air with his long snotty nose, then wiping it on his jacket sleeve.

Stinkerbell scowled. These two Gob brothers were trouble, and trouble she didn't need right now. 'How many times do I have to tell you, *I do not smell of*

bananas!' she said crossly. 'And what do you two idiots want, anyway? Goblins aren't allowed in Charm School. Don't you have your own school. Now, what's it called?' Stinkerbell put her finger to her mouth and pondered. 'Oh, I know,' she said brightly, 'DIM School. That's it. Dim dim dimmy school. Now go away the pair of you because I'm busy learning fairy-type things.'

'You're not a proper fairy. Never were and never will be, Stinks,' said Dwayne Gob nastily. 'Real fairies don't go around blowing up their teachers with their wands. Me and Elv got two weeks detention for less than that. Two weeks every night after school for spray painting "A GOB NEVER FORGETS" on the side of a number seven bus – *and* we had to clean it off as well.'

Stinkerbell looked at each brother in turn. 'I did not blow up Miss Primslip on purpose. It was an accident,' she said. 'And anyway, she's back to normal now, and I did apologise. And as for you two getting detention, what a load of rubbish. You were kept behind for about ten minutes and then your feet began to smell so much the teacher had to let you go – he almost passed out! The stink was *that* bad!'

'That's not true,' sneered Dwayne. 'We escaped, didn't we, Elv?'

Elvis Gob nodded his head vigorously. 'Yeah. We went over the wall, and we had a getaway car waiting for us.'

'Don't tell fibs,' said Stinkerbell, shaking her head. 'You were so worried about your mummy and daddy finding out that you'd been naughty, you tried to get

back *in* to school! Only the teachers wouldn't let you through the door. In fact, they told you *never* to come back unless you washed your socks. And as for the get-away car, you tried to steal that toy one from the little boy who lives at number twelve, didn't you? And he wailed so loudly when you tried to drive off in it that you both ran away empty-handed. June Bloom, the fairy who lives under the sun-lounger in the garden there told me that the very first word that little boy said wasn't Mummy or Daddy, it was GOB! His parents are most upset.'

The two Gob brothers stared at Stinkerbell. And then Douglas, who had crept up, peeped around the front of her potato-peeling skirt and stammered bravely, 'You shouldn't go around spray-painting. It makes a terrible mess and it's very anti-social. Now why don't you get yourselves a nice pad of paper and some watercolours and go and paint the duckpond in the park instead. I don't know, you boys really do need some direction.'

Dwayne and Elvis sneered at Douglas, and then they grabbed the front of his little woolly hat and pulled it down very firmly over his face.

'Our teacher at Dim School said that,' replied Elvis. 'So we pointed him in the direction of the canal and then we pushed him in. He was off work for two weeks with a stinking cold.'

The Gob brothers whooped with laughter. After a few minutes of hysterics, they managed to compose themselves.

'Actually, we've come to tell you that we're moving,' announced Elvis, looking pleased with himself.

'Good. To another country, I hope,' said Stinkerbell rudely.

Elvis shook his head and his quiff quivered. 'Nah. My mum hates flying. Except of her own accord, of course. Actually, we're leaving the brewery because it's cold and draughty and it's playing havoc with my mum's chilblains, not to mention our hairstyles when the wind whips through in a northerly direction.'

'So where are you moving to, then?' asked Stinkerbell suspiciously.

'We're not allowed to say,' replied Dwayne. 'It's top secret. Our mum said she'd have our guts for garters, whatever they are, if we told anyone. But it's not a million miles from where you normally hang out, Stinkerbell. So you could say that we're going to be neighbours. Great, innit!'

And with that they turned on their heels and, whooping with laughter, raced back across the playground, stopping only to pick up a poor little pixie called Henry and stick him head-first into a nearby litter-bin.

Stinkerbell watched them disappear through the gates and then she turned and frowned at Douglas.

'Supposing, just supposing, Douglas, that the Gobs are moving into my dustbin,' she said, looking worried.

'Elvis will be sleeping in *my* bed. Mr and Mrs Gob will drink that foul-smelling Goblin Guck and drop bits of pickled onion all over *my* kipper-skin rug, and Dwayne will put his big smelly feet on *my* table. I can't let them move in. I can't. *I can't.* I CAN'T!' And she jumped up and down so hard in her clompy boots that the bell on Douglas's hat began to ring.

'But it's just a dustbin, Stinkerbell,' said Douglas with a sigh. 'And it's a mess, anyway.'

Stinkerbell put her hands on her hips and clutched her wand tightly. 'Yes. But it's *my* bin. And it's *my* mess,' she replied firmly. And then without another word she stomped out of the playground with such a determined look on her face that Douglas dared not follow her.

Who's Been Sleeping in My Bin?

WHEN STINKERBELL reached her dustbin in the front garden, she flew up on to the lid and peered cautiously inside.

'Hello. Is anybody there?' she called. But her own tiny voice just echoed back. Her dustbin was practically empty except for her banana-skin hammock, her kipper-skin rug and a milk carton.

Hmm. Now that would make a nice coffee table for a while, Stinkerbell thought, as she flew down to inspect it.

No sooner had she landed, when she heard the strangest noise coming from inside the carton. Someone seemed to be banging on the side of it. Stinkerbell placed her ear against the carton and tapped softly back. Then an echoey, muffled voice said, 'Get me outta here, man!'

'Oh my goodness gracious me! A talking milk carton!' squealed Stinkerbell, jumping quickly back and tripping over her kipper-skin rug. Then she picked herself up, hurried round to the top of the carton and poked her head through the opening.

Inside, it was like a big cave, with white translucent

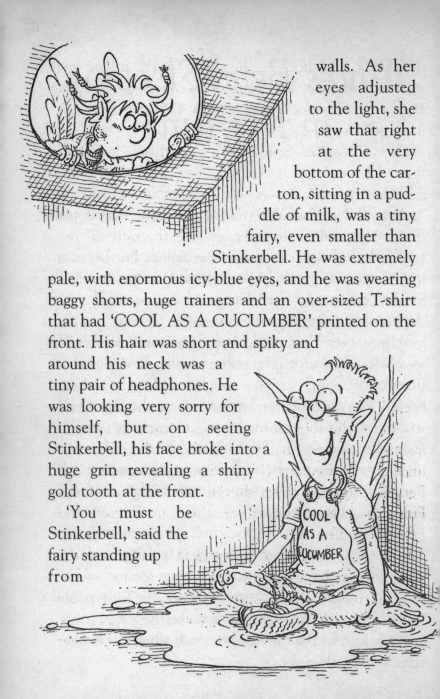

walls. As her eyes adjusted to the light, she saw that right at the very bottom of the carton, sitting in a puddle of milk, was a tiny fairy, even smaller than Stinkerbell. He was extremely pale, with enormous icy-blue eyes, and he was wearing baggy shorts, huge trainers and an over-sized T-shirt that had 'COOL AS A CUCUMBER' printed on the front. His hair was short and spiky and around his neck was a tiny pair of headphones. He was looking very sorry for himself, but on seeing Stinkerbell, his face broke into a huge grin revealing a shiny gold tooth at the front.

'You must be Stinkerbell,' said the fairy standing up from

the puddle. He shook his head and let out a long low whistle. 'Of all of the dustbins in all of world, I get chucked into yours. You're famous, Stinkerbell. A living legend.'

'Am I?' replied Stinkerbell, smoothing down her skirt. 'I haven't got a clue who you are, though,' she said bluntly.

'Yes, well you wouldn't. That's because I don't get out much,' replied the fairy, shaking the milk off the seat of his trousers. 'You see, I'm what's known as a fridge fairy. Do you know what a fridge fairy is, Stinkerbell?'

'Of course I do,' replied Stinkerbell. 'A couple of my friends live in the supermarket freezer in between the ice-cream section and the frozen peas. I don't visit them that often. I have trouble talking to them because my teeth chatter so much. And the last time I was there, the soles of my boots got stuck to a box of frozen fishfingers. I had to leave them off for two days until they thawed out. Do you live in the supermarket? Perhaps you know them, they're called Fred and Freda Frosty. But everyone knows them as Fffffred and Fffffreda Ffffffrosty.'

The fridge fairy shook his head. 'My fridge is in the house,' he declared proudly.

Stinkerbell looked suitably impressed. To actually live inside a human's house was something very privileged indeed in the fairy world. Only a few fairies ever achieved this honour.

'So what are you doing in my dustbin, then?' asked Stinkerbell with a frown. 'Have you been banished to it, like me? Have you done something wrong? I'm *always* doing things wrong.'

'No, it was my mistake,' replied the fridge fairy. 'I was listening to the new "Electric Elves" album on my headphones and chilling out in the milk carton. That's the coolest place to be in the fridge, man. Of course, the freezer upstairs is the very coolest place to be, but I haven't passed enough "cool" exams to move up there yet. Freezer fairies are so cool, Stinkerbell, they make us fridge fairies look HOT HOT HOT!

'Anyway, as I said, I was listening to my music and didn't notice the Big Hand coming into the fridge. You've always got to keep your eyes and ears open for the Big Hand, Stinkerbell. When you're a fridge fairy the Big Hand spells danger. There's a couple of Little Hands as well. They're usually grubby and they *always* go for the sweet things. They're really fast, too. So you learn to stay well clear of the Big and Little Hands. Hand Dodging's one of the first lessons you learn when you become a fridge fairy. But today . . .' Here the fridge fairy shook his head in disbelief, 'Today I just didn't move quickly enough, and before I knew it, the Big Hand grabbed the carton and took a great swig.'

Stinkerbell's eyes widened in disbelief. 'You mean . . . you were nearly . . . swallowed!' She clapped her hand to her mouth.

The fridge fairy nodded solemnly. 'Yeah, man. It's a

good job I can swim because I was very nearly a gonna! I could have ended up in that great big freezer cabinet in the sky! But anyway, I could feel the Big Hand carrying me out of the front door and down the path. It took one more swig and I was hanging on for dear life when suddenly I was flying through the air and finally ended up in here. Lucky escape or what, man?"

The fridge fairy mopped his brow on the sleeve of his T-shirt. 'But I've got to get back in the fridge. It's just too darn hot here. How do you stand it, Stinkerbell?'

'Actually, I always find it a bit draughty. That's because the lid doesn't fit properly.'

The fridge fairy blew through his lips. 'To a fridge fairy, this is *boiling*. But that's not the only reason I must get back inside the Big Hand's house, Stinkerbell. You see, there have been some strange goings-on in the kitchen, and I've got to investigate.'

'Investigate?'

'Yeah. Stuff keeps on being moved about,' said the fridge fairy, 'and there are some weird noises, even when the Big and Little Hands are out for the day. It's real spooky, man.'

'Sounds exciting to me,' said Stinkerbell eagerly. Investigating some spooky goings-on was *much* more interesting than going back to Charm School for the afternoon. 'Come on, what are we waiting for?' she said determinedly. 'Let's go and take a look.' And she picked up her wand and flew up on to the lid of her dustbin.

The fridge fairy emerged from the milk carton, still wearing a pair of pink tinted sunglasses. Stinkerbell had to admit he did look a little on the warm side.

'What's your name by the way?' she asked.

'I'm Chilly,' he replied, flying up to join Stinkerbell, and squinting up at the sun. 'Uh-oh. Look at that rag-

ing ball of fire,' he exclaimed. 'I'm gonna fry. I'm gonna sizzle. I'm gonna shrivel, shrivel, shrivel!'

'Oh don't be so silly, Chilly. It's not *that* hot,' said Stinkerbell. 'Now, just tell me how we get inside the house, and then we can get you out of the sun.'

Chilly pointed towards the front door. 'We go through the litter-box. That's the big hole in the middle of the door that another Big Hand keeps on shoving bits of paper through. Stacks and stacks of it. Don't ask me why. Perhaps it's mistaking the house for your dustbin, Stinkerbell. Anyway I'll need you to prize open the flap with your wand and then we can climb through.'

'OK,' said Stinkerbell eagerly, 'come on.' And she flew off towards the front door, with little Chilly puffing and blowing like a steam train behind her.

Through the Litter-Box

LUCKILY THE flap of the letter-box had been wedged open by a newspaper, so climbing in proved to be very easy.

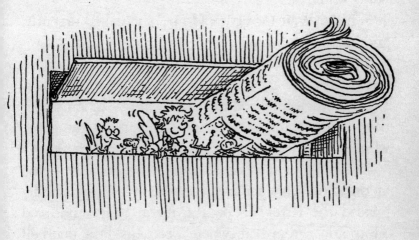

'Oo look. Blue grass. How strange,' remarked Stinkerbell, as she landed with a thud next to Chilly on the hall carpet. 'It's a bit itchy,' she added as she picked herself up and rubbed the back of her potato-peeling skirt.

'Us fridge fairies call it the wide blue river,' said Chilly. 'But the Big Hands call it a *car-pet*. And it stops where our kitchen begins. Come on, I'll show you.'

And he headed off towards the kitchen door.

'Funny sort of pet,' said Stinkerbell, staring down at it. 'I wonder what it eats?' And then she quickly followed Chilly just in case it decided to eat her.

Chilly had reached the end of the hallway and was eagerly entering the kitchen. Suddenly the house seemed very, very, quiet except for the slow ticking of a clock. To Stinkerbell it seemed just a little too quiet, She had the distinct and uneasy feeling that she was being watched.

'Chilly! Wait for little old me,' she called urgently, and hurried after him.

Chilly was staring up in adoration at the enormous refrigerator.

Stinkerbell followed his gaze. 'Oo. It's much bigger than my dustbin,' she remarked looking at the huge, white oblong box. 'And it's an awful lot cleaner, too.'

'Welcome to my home,' said Chilly proudly, flying up on to the work surface. Stinkerbell followed. Chilly pressed the letter 'O' on the metal badge that said 'Hotpoint'. From somewhere deep inside a doorbell rang, and after a few moments the massive door began to open.

Stinkerbell peered in. 'My, my, my, what a lot of food,' she gasped, eyeing the plates of this and jars of that crammed on to the shelves.

'We fridge fairies live on all four floors,' said Chilly, climbing inside.

'Basement is the fruit and vegetable floor. That's me.

24

I'm a fruit and vegetable fridge fairy. First floor is the cold meats and cheeses. That's the level for fridge fairies who've passed their first "cool" exam. Second is drinks, and last night's lasagne or whatever else is left over, and then the top floor is for pickles, salad cream and dressings. Now, to make it to this level means . . .' Chilly pointed a finger towards the ceiling. 'It means that you've almost made it into the freezer, man. But you've got to pass some "cool" exams first.'

'What are "cool" exams?' asked Stinkerbell, sitting down on top of a yoghurt pot and then jumping up immediately because it was so cold. 'Are they easy? I haven't even passed my flying exams at Charm School, that's why I can't fly very well sometimes.'

'There are two exams,' explained Chilly. 'The first is pretty easy. You're given three potatoes and you have to make them disappear for three days and then reappear as tomatoes.'

'Sounds easy peasy to me,' said Stinkerbell, waving her wand about. 'I can make things disappear, you know. Well, half of something, usually,' she added hastily, just in case Chilly asked for a demonstration.

'The second "cool" exam is much harder, though,' continued Chilly.

'To pass this exam means that you are cool enough, and clever enough, and magical enough to move on up to the freezer. But it's tough, man, and a lot of fridge fairies fail and have to try again next year.'

'So what do you have to do?' asked Stinkerbell eagerly.

'Well, you have to conjure up the most amazing ice-cream ever,' said Chilly, his eyes twinkling with excitement.

'It can be any shape or size or colour. But what it most definitely musn't be is boring. No plain old vanilla stuck in a cornet or wedged between two wafers, no

sir-ee. *That* won't earn you a place in the freezer cabinet. You must think of strawberry and chocolate, maybe whipped together. Hundreds and hundreds of hundreds and thousands. Banana flavour. Toffee flavour.

'Cherry, coke and marshmallow flavour. Ice-cream with fruit gums mixed in. Multi-coloured ice-cream. Choc-chip mint with a caramel topping. *That's* the sort of ice-cream you have to create. And then if you pass, you and your creation can move into the freezer, where it stays with you until one day a Little Hand will whip open the door, take it out, and wolf it down in about five seconds flat. All that magic and creativity gone in the blink of a fairy's eye.' Chilly snapped his fingers together and sighed.

'How about a nice banana-and-kipper flavoured one?' suggested Stinkerbell, 'with a sprinkling of tea leaves on top? Do you think that would get me into the freezer? It's delicious. Sometimes I make myself an omelette out of all that stuff.'

Chilly was speechless. Stinkerbell thought he must be impressed. 'So anyway, where are all the other fridge fairies, then?' she asked. 'Have they passed their "cool" exams and moved upstairs?'

'A fridge fairy will *never* show itself when the fridge door is open. It must be shut. Watch.' Chilly pulled out a tiny wand from his pocket, and waved it about, chanting:

'Behind the butter
Under the cheese
Close the door, fairies, and show yourselves please.'

Slowly, the door began to close. As it shut with a

dull thud, they were plunged into total darkness.

'Aah!' screeched Stinkerbell. 'Who put the light out? It's blacker than a mole's hole in here.'

Suddenly the light clicked back on and Stinkerbell saw that she was now surrounded by ten or eleven fairies all staring at her with the same pale blue eyes as Chilly. They were dressed like him as well, though each T-shirt had something different written on it like 'FAR OUT FAIRY' or 'KEEP YOUR

COOL, FAIRIES RULE'.

'Goodness!' exclaimed Stinkerbell, jumping back with a start. 'You didn't half make me jump.'

Chilly introduced his fridge friends to Stinkerbell and she shook each icy hand in turn.

'I thought for one moment that you all had to live in the dark,' she said, blowing on her frozen fingers.

'Hey, no!' laughed a fridge fairy whose T-shirt had 'SUITABLE FOR HOME FREEZING' printed boldly on the front. 'The Big Hands think that every time they shut the fridge door the light stays off. But little do they know that we fridge fairies just go right ahead and switch it straight back on again. Those Little Hands are sneaky, though. They're not so sure, and they sometimes try to catch us out by almost shutting the door and peeking through the crack. But we're smart. They haven't caught us yet.'

Stinkerbell smiled and pulled her silver jacket a little tighter around her. 'So you never suffer from runny noses, or frost-bite in your tootsies, then?' she asked, trying desperately to stop her teeth from chattering.

A fairy called Thaw, whose hair was as yellow as the chunk of butter he was sitting on, shook his head and laughed loudly. 'You think *this* is cold, Stinkerbell?' he said in amazement. 'No way, man. Just go and take a look in the freezer upstairs where Ice and the freezer fairies live – Now *that's* cold.'

'Who's Ice?' asked Stinkerbell, clomping up and down so hard to keep warm that she made a bowl of jelly quiver uncontrollably. The fairy called Nippy who was sitting on top of it shook from head to toe.

'Ice. Or Mr Icicle, Iceberg, Ice-Lolly to use his full name,' replied Thaw excitedly. 'He's the coldest, coolest fairy in *any* freezer *anywhere*. Be it chest, cabinet or storage. From England to Iceland. From America to Antarctica. He's Mr Breeze, he's darn near the coolest fairy you'll *ever* see. Some of his spells, they're wicked, man. And the ice-cream that he created to move into the freezer was so magnificent it's been included in the *Big Babalula Book of Spells and Trickery*.'

'Wow! That's the oldest fairy spell book in the whole wide world,' said Stinkerbell. 'You've got to be *really* good at making up spells to get into *that*. I don't suppose I'll ever get a mention in it, 'cause all my spells seem to go wrong.'

'Never mind, Stinkerbell,' said Chilly, putting his arm around her, 'why don't you come upstairs and meet our freezer friends?'

'Don't mind if I do,' replied Stinkerbell, perking up instantly. And she followed Chilly and Nippy out of the fridge and up on to the freezer handle.

Chilly pressed the other 'O', and as the door opened, they were greeted by an amazing sight. A group of frosted fairies all covered in a thin layer of ice were staring at her. Their hair was so frozen it stuck up in all directions, and their clothes were as stiff as cardboard.

In the middle of them was Mr Ice-Lolly, clad from head to toe in glorious silver; silver boots, silver suit

31

and on top of his head he wore a crown of icicles. Even his hair was silver and it shimmered and shone and glistened. But it was his wand that Stinkerbell's eyes were attracted to. It was the most magnificent wand she had ever seen. It was made out of solid ice, with a cluster of hundreds and thousands of multi-coloured jewels spilling over the top and down the sides, and it looked exactly like an ice-lolly on a stick.

There was a swirling mist coming from Ice-Lolly, and when he opened his mouth, great clouds of condensation puffed out. 'Well, well, well,' he declared with a smile, showing his frost-covered teeth. 'If it isn't little Miss Stinkerbell. Us freezer fairies have heard a lot about you. I hear that you live in a dustbin and that *you're* the coolest fairy around. Cooler than me, even!' Stinkerbell lowered her eyes sweetly. 'Oh, I'm not too sure about that, Mr Lolly,' she replied modestly. 'But if that's what everyone thinks then . . .' she shrugged her shoulders and gave him a big smile, 'I guess I must be!'

Ice-Lolly looked at her seriously and moved a little closer. 'Well, I'm glad you've come, Stinkerbell. I don't know whether you've heard,' he said quietly, 'but here in the kitchen, some strange things have been happening. At night when the Big and Little Hands are safely tucked up in bed, and during the day when they are all out doing whatever it is that Big and Little Hands do, things are being switched on. The kettle boils, the coffee machine bubbles and yesterday the microwave went *ding, ding, ding* all day long. It was most annoying. There are some other very weird sounds, too. Burps and sniffs and glugging noises. It's very peculiar.'

Ice-Lolly pointed with his wand towards the kitchen sink. 'Why, only this morning I saw some shifty-looking dudes lurking over by the cutlery drawer. I couldn't quite make them out because they were hidden behind the pepper grinder. But they looked like they were up to no good. I am just about to go and take a look, maybe see if I can spot some footprints in the sugar bowl or something.'

'Oh, how exciting. Can I come and investigate with you?' asked Stinkerbell eagerly. 'I do love a good nose around.'

'Of course you can. It would be an honour to have the famous dustbin fairy along,' replied Ice-Lolly,

taking Stinkerbell's arm
and leading the way
across the work surface
towards the cutlery drawer,
closely followed by Chilly
and Nippy.

When they reached it, Ice-Lolly tapped the drawer
with his wand and it sprung open. Inside, all the forks
and spoons had been twisted and bent like corkscrews.
Ice-Lolly tutted loudly and shook his head, making a
flurry of snowflakes fall at his feet.

'This is real bad,' he declared gravely. 'A fairy must

never tamper with a Big Hand's tools. Hey! What's this?' He picked up a note that had been hastily written on the back of a torn wine-label.

It said:

'TRY EATIN SPARGETEE OFF OF THEASE.
HA HA HA. HEE HEE HEE.
WE'RE MOVIN IN JUST YOU SEA.'

And it was signed

'What terrible spelling, man,' said Chilly, peering over Ice-Lolly's shoulder. 'And as for that signature. It looks like a baby fairy's scribble.'

Stinkerbell frowned. Taking a look at the note, she was beginning to have an idea who these cutlery wreakers might be.

'I think you might have some new lodgers,' declared Stinkerbell looking at each fairy in turn. 'Have you ever heard of the Gobs?'

As soon as she uttered that dreadful name both Chilly and Nippy went paler than ever. Ice-Lolly stepped back in horror and fell into the sink. As he climbed out, he looked as if he'd seen a ghost.

'I met those Gobs years ago,' he said fearfully. 'That Dwayne and Elvis, they were just goblin babies then. Their mum used to push them around in a rickety old squeaky pram made out of a miniature beer-barrel, and they wore big black binliner nappies and matching black bonnets. And their dummies were made out of bits of wine cork. They were ugly babies, Stinkerbell. And I do mean *ugly*.'

'They haven't changed much, then,' remarked Stinkerbell. ''cause they're still revolting.'

'I was a fridge fairy then,' continued Ice-Lolly. 'And I was living in a house next to the brewery. One day I ventured too far and I met Mr and Mrs Gob out for a stroll with those hideous babies.' Ice-Lolly shook his head. 'I can hardly begin to tell you what they had in store for me.'

'Pickled onion sandwiches? Boring board games?' suggested Stinkerbell helpfully, remembering the time that she had been holed up with them inside the deserted brewery.

Ice-Lolly shook his frosty hair once again. 'They did something that you must never ever do to anyone, especially a fridge fairy.'

Nippy and Chilly looked at each other fearfully as though they knew what he was about to say.

'And what's that, Mr Ice-Lolly?' asked Stinkerbell, looking puzzled.

Ice-Lolly took a deep breath. 'Those Gobs, they brought me back to the house and they put me, a fridge fairy, they put me . . .' Ice-Lolly held an icy hand to his forehead and said dramatically,

'They put me in the OVEN!'

Stinkerbell gasped, and clutched her wand to her chest. 'What happened?'

Ice-Lolly breathed a sigh of relief. 'Well, luckily for me they were too dim to switch it on,' he replied, leaning against one of the taps. 'But I'll always remember that terrible *squeak, squeak, squeak* of those pram wheels as they left me in the dark.'

Ice-Lolly stared at Stinkerbell. 'I tell you, Stinkerbell. Ice has never forgotten it. And now you say those Gobs are moving in.'

'Well it looks that way, Mr Lolly,' said Stinkerbell, hoping very much that she might be wrong. But then suddenly from the direction of the living room a door slammed. Something smashed, and then the all too familiar Gob cackle could be heard echoing around the house.

Stinkerbell and the other fairies turned towards the fridge door, where the brightly-coloured fridge magnets now spelt out:

in big, bold, chunky letters.

Talcum Powder and Toilet Rolls

THE GOBS were having a ball. They hadn't had so much fun since – well, they couldn't even remember.

'Oi, you two. Pass that flat wand thingy over 'ere, will you,' screeched Mrs Gob, pointing to the TV and video remote control.

Dwayne and Elvis stopped unravelling the curtains and dragged the control from the arm of the chair over to Mr and Mrs Gob, who were sitting munching chocolates.

'Ugh! Nut Brittle!' exclaimed Mr Gob, spitting bits of half-eaten chocolate all over Mrs Gob. 'I 'ate nut brittle. Why don't they make pickled onion chocolates. Or Goblin Guck liqueurs.'

Mrs Gob picked a bit of chocolate out of her hair and ate it, then she pressed a button on the remote with a long sticky finger. The television flickered on.

'Oo! My favourite, "Elfenders",' she said, settling down to watch.

'Come on, Elv,' said Dwayne, 'let's have a nose around.'

'Yeah. See where we're gonna sleep and stuff like that,' said Elvis heading off after Dwayne.

Mrs Gob didn't notice them leave, so engrossed was she in her programme.

Mr Gob meanwhile was feeling a bit tired after the move from the brewery. True, he'd only had to carry a carrier bag but even that was too much like hard work for a goblin, so he went to have a snooze inside the video recorder where it was nice and dark and reminded him of home.

Back in the kitchen, Stinker-bell was peeping through the keyhole into the living room.

'What's happening?' whispered Ice-Lolly. 'Are they doing something really bad?' He was glad that Stinkerbell appeared to have taken over.

Stinkerbell flew back down. 'Mrs Gob's watching TV,' she said, 'and Mr Gob's having a sleep. But it looks like Dwayne and Elvis have gone upstairs.'

'Upstairs!' gasped Chilly. 'No one ever goes upstairs. It's out of bounds to a fairy. If the Big Hands come home and find them they'll send in investigators. Fairybusters to flush us out. We're doomed. We'll never find another vacant fridge this side of the country. You've got to get them out of here, Stinkerbell – before the Big Hands get back. They'll be home for tea!'

All the fairies looked pleadingly towards Stinkerbell.

'Hang on. Hang on one teeny weeny minute,' she said, holding up her hands. 'What do you mean *I've* got to get them out? I thought you lot were supposed to be the coolest fairies on the planet. How come you're panicking like a load of demented dormice?'

They looked very sheepish and even Ice-Lolly had lost his sparkle.

'We're only cool when we're in the fridge,' he said forlornly. 'We don't like being outside it.'

Stinkerbell sighed and shook her head. 'You sound like someone else I know. You're not related to a pixie called Douglas are you, by any chance?' She said, thinking what a wimp Douglas had been when she'd rescued him from the Gobs. 'Well, I'll need one of you to come with me, at least,' she said huffily.

None of them looked like they wanted to go anywhere.

Stinkerbell held out her wand. 'Eeany meany miney mo. Catch a fairy by its toe. If it hollers let it go. Eeany meany miney mo.'

The wand stopped at Nippy. Nippy hadn't stopped shaking since she'd jumped off the bowl of jelly. She looked terrified as Stinkerbell put an arm around her shoulder.

'Right, Nips,' she said, giving her a squeeze. 'Looks like it's up to us girls. Come along, we've no time to lose if we're going to save the house from mass Gob destruction by tea-time.' And they headed off towards the stairs with all the fridge and freezer fairies peering around the door and waving after them.

Stinkerbell and Nippy flew up the staircase. There were shrieks and hollers coming from the bathroom. Stinkerbell and Nippy peeped around the door and saw that the place was an absolute mess. The shower curtain was hanging off, an unravelled toilet roll was wrapped around everything in sight, and the sink was filled with bubbles which overflowed on to the floor. Elvis was swinging off the toilet chain like a miniature Tarzan.

'Oh dear. Oh deary, deary me,' whispered Stinkerbell. 'I see those boys are still as terrible as ever. They won't listen to me. I'm going to have to try some magic to make them stop.'

Nippy looked at Stinkerbell's TV aerial wand. 'Oh is *that* a wand?' she asked in amazement. 'I wondered what it was.'

Stinkerbell gave her a dirty look. 'Excuse me,' she said haughtily, 'but I made this all by myself. And I'm very proud of it. Anyway, I don't see you with one.'

Nippy fanned her face with her hand as she was beginning to feel a little warm. 'Us fridge fairies can only do magic when we're inside the fridge. Our powers are useless out here,' she said, looking a bit shameful.

'Oh really?' said Stinkerbell snootily. 'Well that's not much help, is it? Let's just hope my wand is behaving itself today.' And she held it in front of her face and wagged a finger at it. 'Now, listen to me,' she said sternly, 'I need some help, so don't let me down, OK?' And she began to wave it around.

'Right. You'd better stand back, Nippy. I don't use it very often 'cause it's a bit unpredictable. Anyway, here goes!' She took a deep breath, closed her eyes tightly and said:

'Into the bathroom weave your way.

Erase those Gobs, they cannot stay.'

Suddenly there was a puff of thick sooty smoke, and there, looking extremely bewildered, was Douglas. He was holding his maths book in one hand and he had the other raised as if he'd been just about to answer a question in class. He blinked rapidly through his glasses.

'What's happening?' he said, panic-stricken. 'Where am I?'

'You're in the Big Hands' house. My name's Nippy, and I'm very pleased to meet you,' replied Nippy politely.

'Shh, shh,' hissed Stinkerbell. 'I was trying to get rid of the Gob brothers, but somehow I got you instead, worse luck.'

Douglas shook his head despairingly at Nippy, and then pointed at Stinkerbell's wand. 'Oh, Stinkerbell. You've been using *that* thing again, haven't you? It's dangerous and I'm sure it must be illegal. You could have had me sent to the moon or somewhere.'

Stinkerbell scowled. 'Hmm. I'll have to remember that next time.' Having dreary Douglas around was about as much help as a chocolate fireguard.

Douglas ignored her. 'What are you doing here, anyway? You're supposed to be in Charm School,' he said, looking around nervously. 'Miss Primslip has told the King of your absence, Stinkerbell, and now he's fuming. Do you know what he said?'

Stinkerbell shook her scruffy plaits, though she had an idea.

'He said, "As soon as that filthy fairy is found she's going straight back into the dustbin". Those were his very words.' Douglas looked seriously at her.

'Oh, never mind about that now,' snapped Stinkerbell. 'I've got a house to save. As soon as the King finds out about my daring deed he'll soon forget all about dustbins. In fact, I wouldn't be surprised if he made me a princess. Then he'll have to give me back my tiara which he's confiscated.' And she went on to explain to Douglas about the events of that morning. But before she could finish, there was the most tremendous clatter from inside the bathroom. Elvis had swung a little too far on the toilet chain and landing on top of the medicine cabinet, had sent boxes and bottles flying through the air. Dwayne, who was standing on the side of the bath, was showered with talcum powder. He peered at himself in the mirror and shook his fist at his brother.

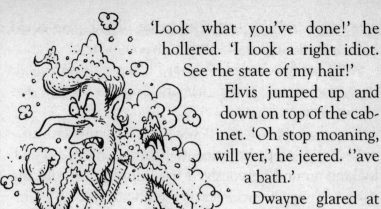

'Look what you've done!' he hollered. 'I look a right idiot. See the state of my hair!'

Elvis jumped up and down on top of the cabinet. 'Oh stop moaning, will yer,' he jeered. ''ave a bath.'

Dwayne glared at him. ''ave you gone stark staring bonkers, bruv? I ain't taking a bath for no one. Washing's for sissys. I'll just have to wait till Mum or Dad can think up a spell to turn me back to black.'

'Please yourself, Snow White,' replied Elvis with a shrug. He flew down to join his brother. As he did so, he looked suspiciously towards the door. 'There's someone out there,' he declared. 'I can smell something.' He sniffed the air. 'Smells like bananas.'

From behind the door, the three fairies tried hard to keep quiet.

'It's no good, Stinkerbell,' whispered Douglas, gripping Nippy's hand. 'Elvis has got a whiff of you. You'll have to go in there, otherwise they might kidnap us again and make us do terrible things . . .

'Still as brave as ever, eh, Dougy dear?' said Stinkerbell sarcastically, and she began to push the door open.

'*You're* very brave, Stinkerbell,' gasped Nippy.

'Yes I am, aren't I?' Stinkerbell said, and she stepped inside.

Trapped

'COOEE!' STINKERBELL called, in her friendliest voice. 'Only me.'

'Who's me?' snapped Dwayne.

'Why, your old mate Stinkerbell, of course,' replied Stinkerbell, moving a little closer.

'Stinkerbell!' exclaimed Dwayne. 'What are you doin' here?'

'Well,' said Stinkerbell, putting her hands behind her back and scrapping her big boots nonchalantly on the bath mat. 'I thought I'd come and welcome you into your new home.'

Elvis eyed her suspiciously. 'Why?' he snapped. 'We hate you. And you hate us.'

'Oh, how could you say such a thing, Elvis dear,' Stinkerbell said innocently. 'I have a very soft spot for both of you.'

Dwayne smoothed back his white quiff. 'Is that right, Stinks?' he said, adjusting his bootlace tie.

'Well, you're not so bad yourself – for a fairy, that is,'

47

he added hastily. 'At least you're dirty and you don't mind staying that way. I know you smell a bit funny, but how about coming out with me sometime? We could go gob-cart racing or to the chip shop if you fancy it?'

Elvis looked at him as if he'd gone quite mad. 'Dwayne!' he snapped. 'Pull yourself together and don't be so soppy.'

Dwayne looked embarrassed. 'Only joking,' he said quickly.

Stinkerbell breathed a sigh of relief. The last thing she needed was a love-struck goblin mooching over her. She frowned at him.

'Dwayne. What on earth have you done to yourself? You look like a snowman.'

'My bruvver knocked talcum powder all over me!' replied Dwayne sulkily.

'I'll get it off,' said Stinkerbell. 'I can turn you back to black just like that.' And she snapped her fingers.

'Oh yeah. How?' asked Dwayne. 'You're useless at spells. Everyone knows that.'

'No, no, no. You're mistaken,' laughed Stinkerbell a little uneasily. 'I'm *much* better since I've been at Charm School. Let me show you what I can do.'

Elvis Gob pulled out his comb and whipped it through his hair. 'Go on, then,' he said. 'But I don't believe a word.'

'Right, here goes,' said Stinkerbell. 'But first could I ask you boys to stand well back.'

Dwayne and Elvis stepped back.

'Just a bit further, if you don't mind. My wand only works over long distances, you see.'

The two Gob brothers stepped back again.

'Back a bit more. Back, back.'

Dwayne and Elvis grudgingly stepped further back and then disappeared as they tumbled off the bath and into a large pink plastic laundry basket. As quick as a flash, Stinkerbell flew up and pushed the lid firmly on. She clapped her hands together.

'There!' she declared triumphantly. 'I told you I'd sort you out. All you have to do now is wait there until a Big Hand comes to do a wash, and then you'll come out as good as new, Dwayne.'

Dwayne and Elvis surfaced through a sea of knickers,

socks and shirts. They clutched the slats of the basket and pressed their faces up against the holes like prisoners.

'You've tricked us again!' roared Elvis, his face crimson with rage.

'Right first time,' Stinkerbell said, giving them a wave and skipping towards the door. 'Now, you boys stay there and make yourselves comfy, until I can figure out how to get rid of you and your mummy and daddy for good. Ta, ta!'

Stinkerbell was just about to step into the hall when Elvis called her back.

'Just remember, Stinkerbell, you filthy fairy,' he said, clutching the bars even tighter with his bony hands. 'A GOB NEVER FORGETS.'

Back on the landing, Nippy and Douglas were waiting eagerly.

'Oh, Stinkerbell,' gasped Nippy. 'You are brave. So all of those stories about you are true, then?'

'What stories?' asked Stinkerbell suspiciously.

'About how you tricked the Gobs and saved the royal fairy baby from their terrible clutches,' continued Nippy, looking at Stinkerbell adoringly with her enormous pale blue eyes.

'Oh *that* story,' said Stinkerbell, looking relieved. 'Yup. It's *all* true. All in a day's work for Stinkerbell.'

Douglas frowned at her. He hated it when Stinkerbell got too big for her already too-big boots.

'Anyway, I've taken care of Dwayne and Elvis for a

while. You stay here, Nippy, while Douglas and I go and see what Mr and Mrs Gob are up to.'

'Do you think you can get them to leave, Stinkerbell?' asked Nippy, watching Stinkerbell fly downstairs, with Douglas following reluctantly. 'Because if you do, the fridge and freezer fairies will be so pleased, that I'm sure you could become one of us.'

'That's very thoughtful of you, Nippy,' said Stinkerbell, resting for a moment against the bannister rail. 'But living in sub-zero temperatures all year round doesn't really appeal to me. You see, I want to be a princess. I want to be the dirtiest, filthiest princess in the whole neighbourhood.'

Stinkerbell flew down to the hall and waited for Douglas. She pushed up the sleeves of her jacket and smoothed down her skirt.

'And I reckon that if I can get rid of the Gob family, I deserve to be made a princess. In fact, the King might even let me become queen. Imagine, Stinkerbell, Queen of the dustbins!'

For a moment Stinkerbell went all dreamy-eyed, but she was soon brought back down to earth by the loud screams of Mr Gob, coming from the direction of the living room.

''elp. 'elp!' he cried. 'I'm being eaten alive!'

Stinkerbell and Douglas looked at each other and wondered what on earth could be gobbling up Mr Gob!

Monsters in the Machinery

STINKERBELL RACED into the living room. Mrs Gob was snoring like a pig, her head resting on the 'Eject' button of the remote control. This was causing Mr Gob grave problems. Having fallen asleep inside the video recorder, he was now sliding in and out of it at great speed.

His jacket had got caught, and every time he emerged with his legs and arms flying wildly about he would shout,

''elp! 'elp! It's got a hold of me! It's gonna swallow

me whole! 'elp! 'elp!' before disappearing back inside.

Stinkerbell flew over to the video and calmly switched off the machine.

Mr Gob hung off the video-flap panting heavily. 'Why, if it isn't that dustbin fairy,' he exclaimed breathlessly. 'What are you doin' here, girl? Shouldn't you be up to your neck in rubbish, or something?'

'Mr Gob,' replied Stinkerbell sternly, hands on hips. 'I have just saved your life. Have you never heard of the Goggle-Eyed monster?'

Mr Gob shook his head and looked shifty.

Stinkerbell pointed with her wand towards the TV set. 'It lives inside there,' she said. 'And it catches fairies in its mouth through there.' She pointed back down to the video. 'That's what it lives on, you see. Fairies, elves and pixies. But it's especially fond of goblins 'cause they're a bit chewier than us lot.'

Mr Gob looked dumbstruck. 'Is that a fact?' he said, glancing over his shoulder. 'Get me out, Stinkerbell, will yer,' he said nervously. 'I'm not ready to be gobbled up just yet.'

Stinkerbell looked up at him. 'Mr Gob, I can only help you if you promise me one thing.'

'Anything. Just name it,' replied Mr Gob, his face as white as a fridge fairy.

'Well, you and your wife, and of course your two sons, must leave this house and find somewhere else to live,' said Stinkerbell firmly. 'I'm sure there must be somewhere more suitable, like an old public convenience or a sawdust strewn corner of a rabbit hutch. Maybe you could move into that hamster's cage at number four. A life behind bars would suit you fine.'

Mr Gob nodded his head vigorously. 'OK, OK,' he said eagerly. 'Just get me out, Stinkerbell, and we'll be gone quicker than a goblin up a drainpipe.'

'Promise?' said Stinkerbell uncertainly. She didn't trust these Gobs one bit.

'Cross my heart and hope to fly,' replied Mr Gob.

'OK, here goes,' said Stinkerbell, and waving her wand about, she began to chant:

'Mr Gob is skinny.

There is no meat on him.

Spit him out this instant.

You need a meal less thin.'

Nothing happened.

'Useless!' cried Mr Gob. 'Absolutely useless! I might have guessed it wouldn't work.'

Suddenly from behind them on the settee came a voice. 'Who's making all that racket. Can't a goblin get her beauty sleep?'

It was Mrs Gob. She'd woken up and was feeling a bit sick from all the chocolates she'd eaten.

'Mrs Gob! 'elp me,' said Mr Gob desperately. 'I'm stuck, and this filthy fairy can't get me out.'

'Oh stop making such a fuss, Mr Gob,' moaned Mrs Gob, climbing down from the settee and stomping over. 'You don't need magic to get you free. You just need a good tug.' And she grabbed hold of the bottom

of Mr Gob's trousers and pulled hard. There was a rip as his jacket unhooked itself, but at the same time Mrs Gob also managed to pull down his trousers, and, as Mr Gob landed in a heap on the floor, they crumpled around his ankles revealing a big, baggy pair of washed-out underpants. Mr Gob leapt up and quickly pulled his trousers up.

'Thanks, Mrs Gob,' he said, looking embarrassed. 'I knew I could rely on the wife to get me out of a difficult situation.' And he proceeded to tell her all about the Goggle-eyed monster.

Mrs Gob screeched with laughter and almost fell over. 'She's havin' you on, Mr Gob. There's no such thing. How would a monster fit inside a telly? There's 'ardly enough room for the cast of "Elfenders" in there, let alone all the other programmes that are on.' She folded her arms and shook her head at Mr Gob. 'Honestly, Mr Gob, don't you know *anything*?'

Stinkerbell could not believe her ears. This family really were incredibly stupid! She looked at Douglas, who had up until now kept very quiet.

'Goodness me,' he exclaimed in wide-eyed amazement. 'I didn't know that's where they lived either!'

Stinkerbell shook her head. She was *surrounded* by idiots!

Then Mrs Gob stopped laughing, and looked very serious. 'But there is a monster lurking in the house that we must be careful of,' she said, sneaking a look over her shoulder.

Mr Gob looked fearful and fingered his bootlace tie nervously. 'Where is it, Mrs Gob?'

'It lives in the vacumn cleaner,' replied Mrs Gob. 'And it's got the biggest pair of lungs you ever saw. It doesn't swallow you, though. It *sucks* you up and you get all stretched like a piece of chewing-gum. It happened to a goblin in Glasgow 'cause I read it in *Goblin Weekly*. He came out twice as long. It was terrible, his trousers were up to his knees and he kept hitting his head on the ceiling.'

Stinkerbell listened to this tall tale with disbelief, but she decided to go along with it. 'Um, perhaps you'd better think about moving out after all, then,' she said innocently. 'It would be dreadful if that happened to Dwayne and Elvis. They look peculiar enough as it is.'

Mrs Gob glared at her. 'We ain't movin', Stinkerbell,' she snapped. 'And don't be rude about my gobby boys. They're *bootiful*.'

'Maybe they've been sucked up already,' insisted
Stinkerbell. 'Because where are they, anyway?'

Mrs Gob narrowed her eyes. 'What 'ave you done to
them, Stinkerbell? 'ave you been upsetting them?
'cause if you have—'

'No, no, Mrs Gob,' replied Stinkerbell. 'I wouldn't
do that. I know how special they are to you.'

'Well, I wouldn't say that,' said Mrs Gob crossing her
arms and looking a bit huffy. 'But they're quite handy
to 'ave around, for chores an' stuff. Perhaps I'd better
go and look for them 'cause I'll need someone to go and
nick the tea from the fridge. Otherwise we'll be eating

out of the cat's bowl again.' And she hurried off in search of them.

Mr Gob meanwhile had been foraging around in his carrier bag and had pulled out a huge pickled-onion sandwich that was curling at the edges, and a bottle of foul-smelling, and even worse-tasting 'Goblin Guck' which is a goblin's favourite drink. He took a great big bite and a long swig, then he slooshed it around his mouth, mashed it up, gurgled with it and finally swallowed it.

'Lovely!' he said, wiping his mouth on the side of the armchair and letting out a deafening burp. 'Now, as my wife says, we're not movin'. Monster or no monster. So if you'll excuse me I'm going to build myself a little campfire and 'ave a nice sit-down.'

Stinkerbell jumped up and down in her hefty boots and the bell on top of Douglas's woolly hat began to ring. 'But you promised you'd leave!'

'Only if YOU got me out. But YOU didn't get me

out, Stinkerbell, Mrs Gob did. So buzz off, the pair of you.' –

'But you can't start a bonfire,' she said imploringly. 'It's dangerous, and besides, the place is centrally heated.'

'Look, this is my house now,' said Mr Gob. 'And if I want a campfire, I'll 'ave one. It'll make me feel more at home. I never really wanted to move in here in the first place. I was quite happy in the brewery with an empty beer crate for a bed and a bottle-top for a pillow.'

Stinkerbell and Douglas watched as Mr Gob gathered up some fluff from the carpet and made a pile, muttering to himself, 'I don't know what's come over my wife lately, she's gone soft on me.' Stinkerbell and Douglas thought Mrs Gob was anything but soft! With her long lank hair and sharp winklepicker stilettos she was a hideous sight, not forgetting her ear-splitting cackle which could suddenly be heard bouncing off the wallpaper in every room upstairs.

Stinkerbell and Douglas looked at each other, their eyes wide.

'Nippy!' they both said together.

'Yeah, it is a bit,' replied Mr Gob, 'that's why I'm building a fire.'

But Stinkerbell and Douglas ignored him, and flew up the stairs as fast as their wings could carry them.

Squashed!

MRS GOB was in one of the Little Hand's bedrooms. She was now wearing a smearing of bright red lipstick, various chains and beads around her neck, and from her ears hung some expensive-looking diamond earrings. She'd forgotten all about her missing boys and was now blowing kisses to herself in the dressing-table mirror, and singing 'I'm so pretty, I'm so pretty' at the top of her voice.

On the bed was a long row of teddy bears and other soft toys.

'I don't like the look of them,' whispered Douglas hesitantly, 'especially that big cream bear with the bow around its neck. Just look at the stare it's giving me. My mummy's read me stories about bears that get terribly upset when you sleep in their bed or eat their porridge. He looks like he could be difficult.'

'Stuffed!' sighed Stinkerbell. 'Stuffed. Stuffed. Stuffed!' she repeated wearily.

'There's no need to be rude, Stinkerbell,' said Douglas huffily.

'No, pudding-brain. I mean they're not real, they're all stuffed. Human children have what's known as toys. Things that they can play with. It looks like that's what Mrs Gob's been doing.'

Stinkerbell pointed towards the bed. Squashed

between a one-eared orange dog and a brown teddy bear was Nippy. Her hair had been roughly put into two bunches and she was now wearing a doll's frilly dress, a woolly hat and scarf, and in her hand was a baby doll's bottle. She was as still as any toy on the bed with her eyes staring straight ahead, but she looked very, very hot indeed.

Mrs Gob, who was still admiring her gruesome looks in the mirror, suddenly caught sight of Stinkerbell and Douglas in it and swung around.

'Well, if it isn't little Miss Dustbin and Mr Compost Heap,' she snapped. 'Haven't you gone yet? Or don't you know where the front door is?'

Stinkerbell walked a little closer to the bed. 'We were wondering whether you might consider letting us stay, Mrs Gob,' she said sweetly.

'No chance,' replied Mrs Gob, picking up the huge lipstick container and smearing it all over her lips. What a sight! She looked like she eaten a massive jam doughnut.

'Oh that *does* suit you, Mrs Gob,' lied Stinkerbell. 'It brings out the colour of your eyes. What would you say they were? Slime pond green? With a touch of cesspool brown?'

Mrs Gob puckered up her lips and patted the side of her hair smugly. 'My mum is a real beauty too, you know. She won the most glamorous goblin grandmother contest last year. The judge couldn't believe that she was a hundred and fifty-six, and he said she had the biggest ears he'd ever seen on a goblin before. I suppose that's where Dwayne and Elvis get their looks.

'Well, maybe I could take some of the strain of being a gorgeous goblin housewife and mother off your shoulders and help you around the house?' Stinkerbell went on, trying not to giggle.

Mrs Gob shook her head, making the diamond earrings shimmer. 'That won't be necessary,' she said, pointing to the row of toys on the bed, ''cause I've already picked someone to 'elp me. I'm going to have my very own au apple!'

'Um, don't you mean *au pair*?' said Douglas nervously.

'Well, whatever they're called, I'm going to 'ave one,' snapped Mrs Gob. 'She's going to be the cook, the cleaner and chief Goblin Guck bottlewasher for us Gobs, and *I'm* going to put my feet up, improve my spell techniques and be a gobby of leisure.'

'Which one have you chosen then, Mrs Gob?' asked Stinkerbell with a frown. 'That big pink teddy over there looks like he could pull his weight.'

Mrs Gob shook her head determinedly. 'Nah. That one with the hat on,' said Mrs Gob, pointing a long skinny finger straight at Nippy. 'She reminds me of one of those fridge fairies I met a few years ago.' Mrs Gob giggled to herself. 'Me and Mr Gob put him in the oven. It was ever so funny. I bet *that* warmed him up a bit. Anyway, I've dressed her up into something more *happropriate*.

'Don't you think she looks a picture? Like a proper little skivvy.'

'You can't surely mean *her*?' laughed Stinkerbell,

pointing towards the little fridge fairy with her wand.

Mrs Gob looked at Stinkerbell crossly. 'What do you mean? What's wrong with her?'

'Well, I don't want to appear rude, Mrs Gob,' replied Stinkerbell slyly. 'But she hardly looks cut out for hard work. She's very puny. She looks like she'd have trouble washing her face, let alone the kitchen floor.'

Mrs Gob stuck her bottom lip out sulkily. 'All right, smartypants. Who would you choose, then?'

Stinkerbell put a finger to her mouth and pondered for a while. 'Oo, it's a hard choice. But I think I'd go for the big dolly over there.' And she pointed towards a large, rosy-cheeked doll with long eyelashes. 'It looks very strong. Just look at its chunky legs.'

Mrs Gob stared at it, moving her head from side to side. Then she flew over on to the bed and looked up at its big round face.

'Right, love. Get your bags packed. You're coming to work for us,' declared Mrs Gob, and she pulled the sleeve of its knitted jacket.

'WAH!' went the doll. 'WAH! WAH!' And everyone including Mrs Gob leapt back.

'It's alive,' hissed Douglas. 'And cross.'

Mrs Gob wasn't to be deterred, though. 'I'll give you wah, wah, you cheeky madam!' she snapped. 'Come on.' And she tugged on its bootee.

This time the doll did move. Stinkerbell and Douglas watched in amazement as very, very slowly it began to tip forward. Its big smiling face loomed

towards Mrs Gob, who stood helpless as it wrapped its arms around her and then finally fell face-first with a thud on to the bed, pinning Mrs Gob to the bedspread so all that could be seen were her skinny arms and legs sticking out.

'Do somethin" she squealed. 'My au orange has trapped me! This is no way to treat your mistress.

You're sacked. I want the little one instead, you're too big to be a maid. You wouldn't fit up the chimney.'

'Too late, Mrs Gob,' said Stinkerbell triumphantly, grabbing Nippy's hand and heading for the door. ''Cause she's coming with us.'

Little Nippy was looking very hot indeed. Her face beneath the woolly hat had gone scarlet.

'Oh dear. Oh deary, deary me,' said Stinkerbell. 'You look like you might melt at any moment.'

'I just need to cool down a little,' replied Nippy.

'Perhaps if you sat in the bath and we gave you a shower,' suggested Douglas helpfully. He liked little Nippy. She was a sensitive soul like him.

'Brilliant idea, Dougy,' said Stinkerbell. 'That's the first sensible thing you've suggested since I've known you. Come on.' And she headed across the landing. 'I can check on Dwayne and Elvis at the same time,' she added, pushing the bathroom door open a little and squeezing through.

But the bathroom was empty. The two Gob brothers had escaped. Hanging down from the laundry basket was a pair of tights. Dwayne and Elvis had tied them around one of the bars, squeezed through a hole and shimmied down them like a couple of cat burglars. On the mirror, sprayed in shaving foam was a message:

'Gone to a BEDDER place. Remember. A Gob NEVER forgets.'

Stinkerbell and Douglas helped Nippy into the bath, and together they turned on the cold tap.

Immediately a jet of icy-cold water sprayed out all over a very relieved fridge fairy.

'We'll be back for you, Nippy,' said Stinkerbell.

Nippy did not reply. She was too busy enjoying her freezing-cold shower, imagining that she was back in the fridge, squashed between a nice bowl of trifle and a tub of margarine.

Battle of the Bed

DWAYNE AND ELVIS were on the huge double bed. They appeared to be making some sort of camp. Elvis had dragged a book from the bedside table and had propped it up like a tent.

Stinkerbell and Douglas flew up on to the bottom of the bed and ducked behind a lump in the duvet. Stinkerbell peeped over the top. Elvis was now sitting inside his book tent and Dwayne was marching up and down the pillows as though he were on guard.

'This is where we're gonna live, Dwayne,' said Elvis, leaning back between the pages. 'On the bed, where it's nice and soft and there's plenty of space.'

Dwayne nodded. 'This is great, Elv. I feel like I'm

camping out in the desert. All you can see for miles is that big yellow cover thing.' He put his hand to his forehead and scoured the vast area of the bed.

Stinkerbell quickly ducked back down.

'This is all our land,' said Dwayne triumphantly. 'We've captured it, and I'm not even gonna let Mum or Dad up here. They'll have to find somewhere else to live.'

'That's right, bruv,' agreed Elvis. 'We're big enough to take care of ourselves now.'

'Yes, and ugly enough,' giggled Stinkerbell to Douglas. Only Douglas did not reply because his nose had begun to twitch and he looked like he was about to sneeze.

'Feathers,' he sniffled. 'There are feathers in this duvet. I'm allergic to feathers. Even the sparrows in the garden bring tears to my eyes.'

'Don't you dare sneeze!' hissed Stinkerbell, holding on to the end of his nose.

Douglas tried desperately to hold his breath, but then he let rip with the most almighty sneeze. 'Aaaa! Atichoo!'

Dwayne and Elvis jumped up and down.

'Great slobbering hound dogs!' said Elvis excitedly. 'There's an enemy in the camp. Get the ammunition, Dwayne, quick.'

Dwayne hurried off and returned a moment later dragging a large toothbrush in one hand, and a tube of toothpaste in the other.

'What on earth are those two up to?' asked Douglas, who had recovered from his sensational sneeze. He and Stinkerbell watched as Dwayne held on to the tooth-brush and his brother carefully squeezed a large blob of toothpaste on to the head of the brush.

'Right, Dwayne,' Elvis hollered.

'Ready.' Dwayne pulled the toothbrush back as far as it would go, while Elvis held on to the end.

'Aim,' shouted his brother.

Dwayne held the head with one hand.

'Fire!' Dwayne let the head of the toothbrush go like a catapult and the blob of toothpaste flew through the air and landed with a splat straight on to Douglas's glasses.

A second later another load splattered all over Stinkerbell's face. She licked it off. 'Mmm. It's ever so tasty,' she said. 'Whatever it is.'

Still the toothpaste kept on coming. And the more it landed on Stinkerbell's face the more she was getting a taste for it. 'I'll have to get some of this stuff,' she said to Douglas whose face was now completely covered except for two little holes where he'd managed to wipe his glasses clean.

'I wonder what it would be like on toast?' said Stinkerbell to herself. 'Or maybe in a sandwich with a bit of peanut butter.'

Dwayne and Elvis were getting very cross.

'They're not surrendering,' said Dwayne angrily. 'Maybe we should try some magic to flush them out?'

Elvis nodded, and had a think.(which didn't take him very long because goblins don't like to spend too much time thinking). 'I've got it!' he declared. 'I've seen Dad do this when he sees a tooth fairy walking up the road. He makes the pavement go all wobbly so the fairy's loose change falls out of its pockets, and then Dad goes along and pinches it! It should work. They're bound to surrender. They'll be wobbling so much they'll be feeling too sick to do anything else!'

Elvis began to wave his arms wildly in the air and leap all over the place. '*One for the money*,' he sang. '*Two for the Gobbys. Now make this cover go all wobbly.*'

Suddenly the duvet became like a huge yellow sea

and Stinkerbell and Douglas were tossed about like corks in an ocean.

'Ugh. I feel sick,' groaned Douglas, bobbing about helplessly. 'Can't we just surrender, Stinkerbell? I think I'd rather eat pickled onion sandwiches for the next ten years than put up with this.'

'Never,' declared Stinkerbell, her potato-peeling skirt flying up in the air as she did a somersault. 'I think I might have an idea, though. Douglas, hold on to my feet.'

Douglas grabbed hold of Stinkerbell's boots and held them tight. Stinkerbell leant across the bed and faced the dressing table. Then she held her wand out in front of her and closed her eyes tightly.

'What are you doing, Stinkerbell?' cried Douglas, clinging on to the soles of her boots for dear life. 'This is no time to have a lie-down'

'I'm not,' Stinkerbell shouted back. 'Watch.' And a moment later there was a ping, and a ding and the bottle of perfume that had been on the dressing table was now standing in front of them. Stinkerbell quickly pulled the lid off and then very carefully, like an acrobat, climbed on to the spray top.

'Now what are you up to? wailed Douglas. 'Why care about how you smell at a time like this? It's never bothered you before.'

Stinkerbell ignored him and with grim determination started to jump up and down as hard as she could on top of the spray.

'Phew. What's that terrible smell?' spluttered the

Gob brothers as a fine mist of perfume wafted their way.

'I've never smelt anything so horrible,' said Elvis, holding on to his long pointy nose. 'Is that you making that pong, Stinkerbell?'

Stinkerbell jumped on the bottle again and the powerful aroma once more drifted towards the Gobs.

'OK, OK. We surrender,' said Dwayne, 'only just stop that *stink*, Stinkerbell. What on earth is it, anyway?'

Stinkerbell jumped back down and peered closely at the label. 'It's human perfume and it's called, "Evening in Paris",' she declared loudly.

'"Evening in Paris"?' scoffed Elvis, wrinkling up his nose as Stinkerbell trudged across the bed towards him.

'It smells more like "Lunchtime in London".' And he looked very nervously at her wand which she held out in front of her.

'You've won for the time being,' sneered Elvis. 'But you haven't heard the last of us.'

'I've got to hand it to you, Stinkerbell,' said Dwayne. 'You're pretty *tuff* for a fairy. Sure you don't fancy hooking up with us and joining our gang?'

Stinkerbell put her hands on her hips. 'What gang? Or do you mean you and your brother?' she said, shaking her head and looking at each of them in turn.

Dwayne looked a bit sheepish. 'Well if *you* joined then there'd be . . .' And he counted slowly on his fingers. 'Three!' he declared brightly.

'No chance,' replied Stinkerbell bluntly. 'Now come on, you two gormless Gobs, we're going downstairs and you can leave through the catflap, 'cause I bet that's the way you came in.'

Dwayne and Elvis sneered at her and sulkily followed her downstairs.

Soaked!

DOUGLAS WENT to fetch Nippy.

She was feeling much better after her good soaking under the cold tap, and she felt even more relieved when Douglas told her about the Gobs' capture. They flew downstairs and into the kitchen. Stinkerbell was escorting the Gob brothers across the kitchen. The fridge door was open, and Ice-Lolly, Chilly and the other fridge fairies were nervously waiting inside.

Ice-Lolly was pacing up and down on a stick of celery. When he saw Stinkerbell and the others heading towards him he looked overjoyed. 'You're safe,' he cried. 'And you've captured the Gob brothers,' he added with a shudder and stepped back into the vegetable compartment. 'Stinkerbell, you are amazing.'

'Well, if you say so,' said Stinkerbell coyly. She glanced at Douglas and Nippy who were now standing beside her.

'Here's Nippy back safe and sound,' she said. 'Oh, and this is Douglas. He lives in the garden, and we go to the same school – but he's not my friend,' she added hastily.

Nippy flew up into the fridge. Ice-Lolly put his arm around her and grinned at Douglas. 'Nippy, I think it's time you became a freezer fairy. You've been very brave to go outside today and help Stinkerbell.'

Nippy shook her head. 'I didn't do anything,' she said quietly. 'I just got very, very hot.'

'Nonsense,' replied Stinkerbell forcefully. 'You kept a cool head, Nippy, even when you had to dress up in those stupid dolly's clothes. I'm proud of you, and you certainly deserve to be frozen solid if that's what you want.'

'And what about you two? Would you like to come and live in the fridge with us?' Chilly asked Stinkerbell and Douglas.

'Oh no, thank you,' replied Douglas. 'I hope to be in charge of the compost heap in the corner of the garden by Christmas. And apart from that, I suffer terribly from colds. But it was kind of you to ask.'

'I don't suppose there's any chance that we could become fridge fairies, is there?' asked Dwayne hopefully.

'We're quite used to being cold, coming from the brewery,' Elvis put in, standing on tiptoe to try and get a better look inside the fridge. 'It looks very nice in there, and we promise to behave ourselves, honest.'

'You have got to be joking, man,' said Chilly. 'You Gobs, apart from being liars, cheats and bullies, just aren't COOL enough.'

Dwayne and Elvis looked furious, but before they could reply there was a grumpy voice behind them.

'So this is where you all are!' It was Mr Gob, who'd shuffled into the kitchen wearing his winklepicker slippers. 'I 'ate this place,' he said, scratching the back of his trousers wearily and looking very sorry for himself. 'You can't even make a decent bonfire. It keeps going out 'cause there's no draught, see. Where's Mrs Gob? I want to go back to the brewery.'

'I'm 'ere,' said Mrs Gob, and everyone turned around to see a very red-faced goblin. She was still wearing the smudged lipstick and looked like she'd been dragged

through a hedge backwards.

'You would not believe what happened to me, Mr Gob,' she said shakily. 'I was nearly smothered by a giant baby. I'm telling you, this house is *full* of monsters, and apart from that I don't like the colour of the wallpaper. So come on, you lot, we're going 'ome.'

'Hoo-flippin-ray,' said Mr Gob hurrying off. 'I'll get me stuff.'

The fridge fairies breathed a cloudy sigh of relief.

'Now perhaps we can get back to normal,' said Ice-Lolly, pressing the O on his freezer door to be let in. 'Us fridge and freezer fairies don't like things in the kitchen to be too hectic. We just like to hang out amongst the food, chill out against a can of something cold, and do absolutely NOTHING!'

Dwayne and Elvis glanced at each other. It was the magic words 'do absolutely nothing' that set them off. They waited until Stinkerbell's back was turned and then as quick as a flash they flew up on top of the fridge.

'Well, what a shame, my frosty friends,' declared Elvis, ''cause me and my brother have decided that *we* want to move in here. We're too old to be living with our mum.'

Mrs Gob put her hands on her hips and stared up at them crossly. 'Dwayne! Elvis!' she shrieked. 'Get down here this instant and pack your things. Whoever heard of a goblin livin' in a fridge.'

'No!' said Dwayne jumping up and down on a cling-film-covered bowl like it was a trampoline.

'Shan't!' said Elvis and he poked his tongue out.

Mrs Gob was fuming. The fridge and freezer fairies peered out to see what all the trouble was.

'If you don't come down, I'll turn you both into a couple of salt and pepper pots and you'll spend the rest of your days being tipped on your head!' roared Mrs Gob.

But even this didn't deter Dwayne or Elvis, for then they did the most terrible thing. They jumped on to the floor, flicked the switch by the fridge, and pulled the big white plug from its socket.

'Whoops!' said Dwayne as they swung it between them. 'We seem to have cut you off.'

The fridge fairies were hysterical, and the freezer fairies became uncontrollable, as from somewhere deep inside the fridge an alarm sounded and a voice boomed out from the cheese compartment: 'Power breakdown! Power breakdown! Abandon fridge! Abandon fridge! Temperature's rising, man. Coolest fairies first!'

Stinkerbell, Douglas and Mrs Gob stood in the middle of the kitchen as all around them there was absolute chaos. Fridge and freezer fairies leapt from all levels wearing inflatable jackets.

'Oh dear. Oh deary, deary me,' declared Stinkerbell watching a puddle emerge from beneath the fridge. 'I think we'd better get out of here, Douglas. I can't swim.'

'Me neither,' replied the little pixie, and they headed towards the catflap with a pool of water lapping at their heels. As they climbed through and tumbled out on to the patio, they could just hear Mrs Gob's voice screeching over the sound of the alarm:

'Dwayne. Elvis! Get down off that fridge. We'd better hide in here!'

Then Dwayne's voice could be heard. 'Mum! Mum! You're pulling my ears off! Let go of them!' Followed by Elvis, 'We didn't mean it, Mum. Honest, Mum. I didn't mean to poke my tongue out, Mum. Och! My nose!'

Then finally everything went quiet. Stinkerbell peered back through the catflap. She could see a long line of fridge and freezer fairies heading up the hall towards the front door. 'Looks like the fairies are going through the litter-box,' she said. 'But I can't see the Gobs anywhere.'

Douglas did not reply. Instead he let out a great big sigh and nudged Stinkerbell. She turned around and came face to face with the King of the garden.

'Oh dear,' said Stinkerbell sheepishly. 'Oh deary, deary me.' And she gave him a cheeky grin. 'Hello, your Majesty. How are you today?' she asked sweetly.

'I was fine until I heard about you,' replied the King, glaring down at her. 'What have you been up to? Miss Primslip tells me you missed Charm School.'

'But I had my reasons, your Majesty. I was saving the house from the invasion of the Gob family.'

The King looked at her doubtfully and then peered through the catflap himself.

'Yee Gads!' he roared. 'What on earth have you done in there, Stinkerbell. I've never seen such a mess! Right, that's it. You've gone too far this time. Making mischief in the garden is one thing, but breaking and entering a human's house – that really is the limit.'

Douglas put up his hand nervously. 'But, your Majesty it's not—' Before he could finish, the King interrupted him. 'And as for you, Douglas, I thought you had more sense. I asked you to keep an eye on Stinkerbell, not join in with her shinanigans! This really could hinder your compost-heap chances, you know.'

Douglas looked like he was about to cry, and

Stinkerbell tried to protest, but the King held his hand up.

'Stinkerbell, I have just one thing to say to you.' And he pointed his wand in the direction of the back gate. Collect your things and GET BACK IN THAT BIN!'

The Biggest Window in the World

STINKERBELL TRUDGED across the garden, dragging her battered wand behind her. She went through the holly bush, and under the garden shed. She pushed open a small creaky door which led into the dormitory she'd shared with the other fairy boarders at Charm School.

Stinkerbell sat at the end of her bunk bed and swung her legs backwards and forwards. It seemed as if she was destined never to stay down at the bottom of the garden for very long. Every time she tried to help, something always seemed to go wrong. And the dream of becoming a filthy fairy princess was becoming more and more remote.

Stinkerbell let out a great big sigh that was bigger than she was, and then, gathering up what few possessions she had, closed the dormitory door behind her and made her way back across the garden. Nobody even bothered to say good-bye, except Douglas, who stopped watering his plants and gave her a little wave.

'Bye, bye, Great Grinning Ones,' she said, as she passed the two garden gnomes by the fishpond. She pulled her jacket a little tighter around her as she reached the washing line.

'And now it's started to rain,' she sighed to herself.

'My dustbin leaks, that's all I need.' And she looked up. But it wasn't raining at all. It was the washing line, now covered with sheets and clothes. Stinkerbell could hardly believe her eyes as there, pegged up between a vest and a pair of knickers, were the Gob family hanging out to dry. In fact, Mr Gob had even been hung upside down.

Stinkerbell tried hard not to giggle, they looked such a sight. Even worse than normal. Their quiffs had lost their quiver and now hung down limply. Their trousers had shrunk, and their winklepicker shoes were so curled up at the toes they looked like Ali Baba's slippers. Even Elvis's bootlace tie had snapped in half.

'Oh dear. Oh deary, deary, me,' said Stinkerbell, trying to avoid the drips that fell off the end of Mr Gob's nose. 'What happened to you lot?'

'We've been pre-washed, washed, rinsed, spun, rinsed and then spun again!' wailed Dwayne.

'We hid inside the washing machine,' said Mrs Gob, struggling against the pull of the pegs. 'I thought we'd be safe in there, but then someone starts piling a load of dirty washing on top of us. It was 'orrible, we got soaked, and Mr Gob got caught up inside a trouser pocket. Tossed around like nobody's business, he was. He's got a terrible headache and now they've gone and hung 'im upside down.'

Elvis Gob glared at Stinkerbell. 'This is all your fault, Stinkerbell,' he said angrily. 'If you hadn't poked your grubby nose in, in the first place, me and my bruvver could have been living in the fridge by now.'

'I was just helping the fridge fairies,' replied Stinkerbell sternly. 'Even you Gobs should know they're the only fairies allowed to live inside a human's house. And apart from that, they're afraid of you lot, though I can't think why, 'cause I'm not.' And she gave them a cheeky grin. 'But what puzzles me is how the humans didn't see you,' she added with a frown.

Dwayne looked down at her sulkily. 'One human did see us, only she thought we were cuddly toys. That's the word she used – CUDDLY! I 'eard her say it as she pegged me up here. 'Oh no,' she said, 'not more CUDDLY toys,' and then she said we was ugly! What a cheek!'

Mr Gob sneered at Stinkerbell as another drip plopped off the end of his nose.

''elp us get down, Stinkerbell,' pleaded Dwayne. 'I feel a right wally up 'ere.'

Stinkerbell shook her head. 'It serves you right,' she said scornfully. 'Maybe if you stay up there for long enough you might see the error of your ways. Bye-bye.' And she skipped off towards her dustbin, happy at least that the Gobs were out of the house and the fridge fairies could continue living a cool and peaceful life inside the refrigerator.

Elvis and Dwayne shook their fists at Stinkerbell. 'We won't forget this, Stinkerbell,' they hollered after her. 'We'll get our own back. It may be tomorrow, the day after, or next week, but we will, 'cause just remember A GOB NEVER FORGETS!'

Stinkerbell turned around and blew them a cheeky kiss. 'Hang on in there, boys, I hope you don't shrink too much,' she called.

When she reached her dustbin, Stinkerbell flew up on to the lid. 'Well,' she said to herself, 'I think that's

enough excitement for one day.' And she clambered inside.

As she did so, she leapt back in amazement, for staring up at her were about twenty pairs of icy-blue eyes surrounded by packets of frozen food.

'Nice pad,' said Ice-lolly who was lying on her banana-skin hammock with an ice pack on his head. 'But a bit bare.'

'That's because it was emptied this morning,' said Stinkerbell, flying down and trying to find a space to sit. She finally wedged herself between Chilly and a packet of oven chips.

'Why aren't you back in your fridge?' she asked. 'You can't possibly want to stay here. It's far too cramped, especially when it starts filling up with rubbish.'

'It's melted, man,' said Chilly. 'Out of action for a while. The whole lot started to defrost and we didn't know where else to go. No fridge or freezer in the whole of this street could fit us in. We were lucky, though, 'cause the Big Hand chucked all this stuff in soon after. So we should be all right here for a bit.'

'Oh well,' said Stinkerbell, trying to sound enthusiastic. 'The more the merrier.'

She didn't want to sound rude, but it was a bit of a squash, not to mention cold, now this lot had moved in.

Anyway, she told them all about the Gobs and what had happened to them in the washing machine.

'So I don't think they'll be bothering you any more,' she said. The fairies looked relieved. 'I'm not sure they'll leave me alone, though,' added Stinkerbell with a sigh. 'Now if I was a *princess* they would, but I'm not. I just wish someone could turn me into one just like that.' And she clicked her fingers together.

Ice-Lolly sat up on the hammock. 'I might know someone who can do just that,' he said thoughtfully. 'Have you ever heard of the cinema, Stinkerbell?'

Stinkerbell shook her head.

'Well, it's a place where inside you can look through the biggest window in the world, and see Big Hands and Little Hands and sometimes even fairies pretending to be someone else. It's called a film, or the movies, and it's sometimes known as the silver screen.'

Stinkerbell and the other fairies gathered round eagerly.

'My cousin Bobby is a cinema fairy,' said Ice-Lolly proudly. 'Cinema fairies live inbetween the seats, and behind the huge curtains that cover the window. They eat this strange stuff called popcorn, that looks like rocks. Big Hands spill most of it on the floor, so there's always plenty to go around. They never see the daylight, though, but they don't mind because they spend their whole time watching films and pretending to be like everyone they see through the window. One day they might be cowboys, and the next a spy. My cousin Bobby came to visit me once and he was dressed up as a doctor. Honestly, Stinkerbell, the cinema fairies are always changing character, you never know where you are with them from one day to the next.'

'How about a princess?' asked Stinkerbell, her eyes wide with fascination. 'Do they ever become princesses?'

'I'm not sure,' replied Ice-Lolly. 'But if you'd like to find out, take this.' And from his pocket he pulled out a small brown ticket that had 'ADMIT ONE' stamped on it. 'This will get you into the cinema. The fairy entrance is down the alleyway and through a crack in the fire exit door. You never know, Stinkerbell, you might have your wish come true at last. Everyone thinks that fairies just grant wishes, and don't wish for things themselves. But of course we do.'

Stinkerbell nodded. 'I want to be a princess more than anything else in the world. I want to be the dirtiest, filthiest, SCRUFFIEST, princess EVER.' And she leant back against the chips with a faraway look in her eyes.

'And WE wish that we were back inside the fridge,' said Chilly. 'So let's go and see if it's been switched back on.'

And all the fridge and freezer fairies gathered themselves together and, saying fond good-byes and a big thank-you to Stinkerbell, flew back along the driveway, heading for the litter-box, the wide blue river and the safety of their fridge.

Stinkerbell lay on her hammock and fell asleep, dreaming she was a gigantic princess with a wand the size of a telegraph pole and boots that were so big they could flatten the whole of the Gob family all in one go.

She was woken up the next morning by Douglas. She flew up on to the lid of her dustbin.

'Stinkerbell,' said Douglas eagerly, 'I've come to tell you that I've explained everything to the King and he says that you're forgiven and you can come back down to the bottom of the garden, providing you behave yourself at Charm School, and stop these silly ideas about becoming a princess.'

Douglas put down his watering can and took off his gardening gloves.

'After all, Stinkerbell, you have about as much

chance of becoming a princess as I have of joining the Gob gang.'

Stinkerbell stood up, wiped her grubby face on the sleeve of her jacket, and brushed a twig through her scruffy plaits.

'That's where you're wrong,' she said, looking up the road towards the High Street, 'because I'm off to the cinema this morning.'

'Whatever for?' asked Douglas. 'It's always night time in that place. And I've heard that the cinema fairies are a very strange bunch indeed.'

Stinkerbell flew down on to the pavement, and looked up at Douglas standing forlornly on top of the dustbin lid.

'I'm going to become a princess,' she declared defiantly. 'Or maybe even a queen with the help of this, dear Dougy.' And she held the ticket up. She carefully put it back inside her silver jacket, turned and headed off up the road. When she reached the front gate of number thirteen she looked back at Douglas.

'Don't worry, Douglas,' she called. 'I'll be back!' And she skipped off up the road singing,

'Stinkerbell, Stinkerbell.
Little, little Stinkerbell.
She's grubby, she's filthy,
She's certainly not clean.
She's off to meet some fairies,
Who'll turn her into her dream .'

And as she looked both ways to cross the road, and

then finally disappeared around the corner, Douglas could still hear her singing away at the top of her tiny voice without a care in the whole, wide, fairy world.